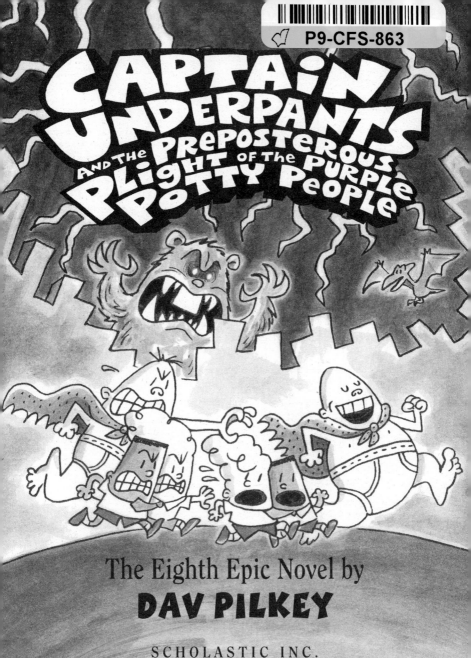

CAPTAIN UNDERPANTS
AND THE PREPOSTEROUS PLIGHT OF THE PURPLE POTTY PEOPLE

The Eighth Epic Novel by
DAV PILKEY

SCHOLASTIC INC.
New York Toronto London Auckland Sydney
Mexico City New Delhi Hong Kong Buenos Aires

This book is being published simultaneously in hardcover by the Blue Sky Press.

ISBN 978-0-439-37614-3 (Trade) / ISBN 978-0-545-38574-9 (BC)

Be sure to check out Dav Pilkey's Extra-Crunchy Web Site O' Fun at
www.pilkey.com.

28 27 26 25 24 23 22 21   19 20 21 22/0

Printed in the United States of America   40

First Scholastic paperback printing, September 2006

For Elizabeth "Boom-Boom" Eulberg
Long live the E.E.C.

CHAPTERS

then they Axident-
eLLy made him ~~think~~
think He was a
super Hero.

You are
captain
underpants

o.k.

Look at me,
I'm Captain
underpants!

HA HA
HA HA

But He exscaped
and ran off to
Fight crime.

TRA-
LA-
LAAA

Rats.

George and Haro-
Ld ran after him.

Hey come
Back Hear

No
way!

Then one day He
drank some super
power Juice.

glug glug
glug

super power Juice

Now He Has sup-
er powers and
stuff.

Lookit Me. I
got super powers
and stuff.

Aw
man!

But if you think thats Bad, it gets worse!

Pay atenchen because this next Part is important!!!

The worst Part is That whenever Mr. Krupp Hears some Body snap Their Fingers...

SNAP

He turns into CAPTAIN Underpants.

Tra·La·Laaa

and whenever somebody splashes water on CAPTAIN Underpantses Face...

H2O

...He turns BAck into Mean oLe Mr. Krupp.

BLaH BLaH Blah

In thier Last advenchure, George and Harold got two New ~~the~~ pets...

a Bionic Hamster named "SULU"...

COOL!

and a pterodactyl named "Crackers"!

awesome!

Everything was cool until this Brainiac Named Melvin showed up.

Im Telling

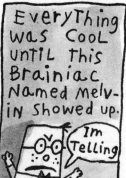

Melvin made a Time machine out of a PURPLE Potty

it Looks Like This.

Anyways, George and Harold wanted to use the Time Machine But Melvin Had one Rule...

Don't use the Time machine 2 days in a ROW!

OK

if you use it 2 days in a Row, So Something very Bad will happen.

OK!

I mean it! Don't use it 2 days in a Row.

OK

sereously! Don't use it 2 days in a row.

OK!

THEN...

Hey, Lets use this Thing 2 days in a Row.

OK

PURPLE POTT CO.

AND SO...

George, Harold, crackers and Sulu used The time machiene 2 Days in a Row... and something Very Bad happened!!!

...WHat WiLL Happen Next?

treehouse comix inc.

CHAPTER 1

GEORGE AND HAROLD

This is George Beard and Harold Hutchins. George is the skeleton on the right with the tie and the flat-top. Harold is the one on the left with the T-shirt and the bad haircut. Remember that now.

As you might remember from our last adventure, George and Harold had recently made the horrifying mistake of trying to pass through a synthetic time warp without letting the C-2X906 super-bimflimanatrix drive of their beebleflux-capacitating zossifyer cool down, thus creating a sub-paradoxical, dimensionalistic alternicon-shift, which opened up a hyper-googliphonic screen door into a sub-omnivating ultra-zinticular bio-nanzonoflanamarzipan.

To put it in scientific terms, *they screwed up*.

But don't get all freaked out because everybody looks like a skeleton. X-ray beams are a normal by-product of inter-dimensional reality shifting. Don't worry, it'll probably clear up by the time you turn the page. . . .

See? What did I tell you?

George, Harold, and their loyal pets suddenly found themselves wishing that they had never set foot inside the petrifying Purple Potty that was about to send them all on a journey into the horrifying abyss of the unknown . . . a journey that would probably spell impending doom for themselves, and would most likely bring about the end of our civilization as we know it. . . .

But before I can tell you that story, I have to tell you *this* story.

CHAPTER 2
THOSE WACKY GROWN-UPS

It's been said that adults spend the first two years of their children's lives trying to make them walk and talk . . .

. . . and the next sixteen years trying to get
them to sit down and shut up.

You're probably wondering, "Why would adults do that? Why would they encourage something one day and *discourage* it the next?"

The only answer I can think of is that adults are totally *bonkers* and should probably be avoided at all times. Perhaps you'll be lucky and find a small handful of grown-ups whom you can trust, but I'm sure we can all agree that you really have to keep an eye on most adults, most of the time.

Which is just what George and Harold did.

It's the same way with potty training: Most adults spend the first few years of a child's life cheerfully discussing pee and poopies, and how important it is to learn to put your pee-pee and poo-poo in the potty like big people do.

But once children have mastered the art of toilet training, they are immediately forbidden to ever talk about poop, pee, toilets, and other bathroom-related subjects again. Such things are suddenly considered rude and vulgar, and are no longer rewarded with praise and cookies and juice boxes.

One day you're a superstar because you pooped in the toilet like a big boy, and the next day you're sitting in the principal's office because you said the word "poopy" in American History class (which, if you ask me, is the perfect place to say that word).

CHAPTER 3
THE SCHOOL OF HARD KNOCKS

Unfortunately, the adults at George and Harold's school were anything *BUT* trustworthy.

Take their principal, Mr. Krupp, for example. Mr. Krupp's wicked heart thrived on the teardrops of children. His very soul danced at the thought of crushing a child's spirit and dashing his or her hopes and dreams against the jagged rocks of never-ending despair.

Each day, Mr. Krupp would stand at
the doorway to his office, gleefully handing
out detention slips to any child who was
unfortunate enough to cross his putrid
path—and for very minor infractions, too,
such as "smiling," "breathing without
permission," or "smelling funny."

24

As bad as Mr. Krupp was, most of the teachers in George and Harold's school were even *worse*.

Fortunately for George and Harold, their evil educators were not very intelligent. They could be outsmarted easily, and they often were.

Now you might think that it wasn't very "sporting" of George and Harold to try and outsmart dumb people, and perhaps you'd be right. But George and Harold were just trying to make the best of a bad situation.

But unfortunately for George and Harold, their bad situation was about to get much, much worse. . . .

CHAPTER 4
PURPLE POTTYVILLE

After several intense minutes of orange flashing lights, X-ray beams, and lightning-infused electric whirlwinds, the Purple Potty finally stopped shaking and sputtering, and came to a sudden halt. Thick yellow smoke poured from its glowing-hot tailpipes as the grinding gears and coughing motor shifted into power-down mode.

George and Harold had no idea what to expect.

They were supposed to be perched high up in a prehistoric tree, 65 million years ago, in the Cretaceous period of the Mesozoic era. But as they stepped out the plastic door of the Purple Potty, the boys were disheartened to find themselves in the middle of the school library, right where they had started.

"What are we doing *here*?" asked Harold.

"I don't know," said George. "Something must have gone wrong."

Harold carefully tucked Crackers back into his book bag, and the two boys looked around the brightly lit library.

"Well, hello, boys," said the school librarian. "This is Banned Books Week. Would you like to expand your minds today?"

"Ummm . . . no thanks," said George.

"Hey," said Harold, "didn't you get fired in our last book?"

"I don't think so," said the librarian.

"Hmmmm," said George. "I'm not feeling very good about this."

"Duh, not feeling good?" asked Melvin Sneedly, who had been struggling to comprehend the easy-to-read children's bestseller, *FrankenFart vs. the Bionic Barf Bunnies from Diarrhea Land*. "Maybe you should go see the school nurse!"

"We have a school nurse?" asked George.

"I thought we just had a box of Band-Aids and a rusty saw," said Harold.

"Duh, of course we have a school nurse," said Melvin. "His office is right next to our five-star gourmet cafeteria."

George and Harold looked confused.

"Uh, *thanks*," said George, "but we'll be O.K."

CHAPTER 5

STRANGERS IN PARADISE LOST

As George and Harold walked down the hallway of their school, they noticed that something seemed wrong. Very wrong. But they couldn't figure out what it was.

IMAGINATION is MORE IMPORTANT THAN KNOWLedge

—ALBERT EINSTEIN

Miss Anthrope, the unbelievably crabby school secretary, passed by the boys and smiled kindly.

"Why, hello, George and Harold," she said. "It's so good to see you two. Have a wonderful day!"

George and Harold looked at her suspiciously.

"Ummmm . . . *what just happened*?" asked Harold.

"I don't know," said George. "But something strange sure is going on."

George and Harold opened their locker
and carefully put Crackers and Sulu inside.

"Shhhh. . . . They're asleep," said George.

"Good," said Harold. "They can take a nap
while we get to class."

On the way to their homeroom, George and Harold stopped to switch the letters around on the lunch menu sign.

TODAY'S MENU:
SOY BURGERS,
HOT LIME PIE,
APPLE JUICE

But just as they were finishing, their principal, Mr. Krupp, caught them red-handed.

"Hey, bubs!" he said. "What are you kids doing out here?"

"Uh . . . ummm . . ." George stammered.
"Y'see, we were ummm . . ."

"Please eat my plump, juicy boogers?"
said Mr. Krupp, giggling with glee. "That's
gotta be the funniest thing I've seen all
day! You boys really crack me up! You're
hilarious!" Then, with a spring in his step,
Mr. Krupp pranced away, whistling a
merry tune.

"Ummmm . . . *what just happened*?" asked Harold.

"Shhhh!" whispered George. "Look!"

George pointed at two kids who were coming toward them, reading a homemade comic book. The kid on the left had a T-shirt and a flat-top. The one on the right had a tie and a bad haircut. Please feel free to remember that now, if you wish.

"It's—it's *US*!" whispered George.

"How can they be us?" whispered Harold. "I thought *we* were us!"

PLEASE EAT MY PLUMP, JUICY BOOGER

George and Harold hid behind a trash can as their two look-alikes walked toward them. They stopped in front of the lunch menu sign and frowned. Then a devilish look came over their faces as they quickly began rearranging the letters.

The strange boys snickered wickedly as they sneaked away from their prank.

"Ummmm . . . *what just happened*?" asked Harold.

"I think I've figured it out," said George.

CHAPTER 6

THE WORLD ACCORDING TO GEORGE

"I think the Purple Potty brought us to some kind of strange, backwards universe," said George.

"No way," said Harold. "That kind of thing only happens in poorly written children's stories whose authors have clearly begun running out of ideas!"

"Here, I'll prove it," said George.

The two friends walked to the cafeteria and took a whiff.

"That's weird," said Harold. "It doesn't smell like dirty diapers, greasy dishwater, and moldy tennis shoes in here anymore. It smells like—like *food*!"

"Yep," said George.

Next, the boys went to the gymnasium.

"That's weird," said Harold. "Our gym teacher isn't fat anymore. And he's not being incredibly cruel to the non-athletic kids like he usually is."

"Yep," said George.

Finally, George and Harold stepped outside.

"That's weird," said Harold. "All of our evilest and most terrifying enemies from the past have been miraculously transformed into good guys."

"Yep," said George.

CHAPTER 7

GETTIN' OUTTA TOWN

George and Harold ran back to their locker.

"Let's grab Crackers and Sulu and get out of this crazy place," said George.

"Good idea," said Harold.

But when they opened the locker door,
their two friends were missing.

"Where the heck are Crackers and Sulu?"
cried George.

"I dunno . . ." said Harold. "Nobody else
has the combination to our locker. Nobody
else except . . ."

"... *our twins!*" gasped George.

Harold tried to shut their locker, but the door jammed on something.

"What's that?" asked George.

"Looks like a comic book," said Harold. He held it up and read the front cover out loud. At that moment, George and Harold began to get a dreadful sense of the horror they were up against.

The PREPOSTEROUS PLIGHT OF CAPTAIN BLUNDERPANTS

By Harold Hutchins and George Beard

Once upon a time, There lived two evil children named George and Harold.

I'm bad.

I am bad as well.

They had a very nice principal who went by the name of MR. KRUPP.

Hello, boys. Have a pleasant day!

Whatever.

One day, George and Harold hypnotized MR. KRUPP.

YOU WILL OBEY US!

Yes, MASTER.

They made him Think he was an evil villain.

You ARE now CapTain Blunderpants.

ALRighT.

George and Harold made Captain BLunderpants Do all sorts of evil Things...

Steal us a video game System.

O.K.

...And Captain BLunderpants Obeyed.

TOYS

GAME STATION 2000

CRASH

Steal us a Big-Screen Television.

O.K.

GAME STATION 2000

AUDIO-VIDEO

CRASH

I'm So happy, I could cry!

me, Too!

Uh-Oh!

GAME STATION

GROCER

TISSUES

CRASH!

AND SO... PIZZA

CRASH

Hold it Right There, CAPTain BLUNDERPANTS!

PIZZA

You've stolen TVs, Jacuzzis, pop mach-ines, Massage chairs, and Disco Balls, but This time you've Gone too far!

You're under arrest for Grand-Theft-Pizza!!!

You've got to catch me first.

ZIP

And the chase was on.

PIZZA

Soon Captain B. was chased onto the freeway.

PIZZA

EPILOGUE

OH, By The way... Whenever CAPTAIN BLUNDERPANTS HEARS Someone SNAP his Fingers...

SNAP

...He TURNS BACK into MR. KRUPP.

Have a swell day!

And Whenever MR. KRUPP GETS WATER on his head...

H₂O

...He TURNS BACK into CAPTAIN BLUnderpants.

GRRR.

REMEMBER THAT, NOW!

EViL TREE House COMiCS, LLC.

CHAPTER 9

NOT WITHOUT MY HAMSTER (. . . AND MY PTERODACTYL)

"I think our evil twins made this comic book," said Harold.

"They must have," said George. "The art-work is really bad, and I'm pretty sure they misspelled some words."

"Let's get out of here," said Harold.

"Not without Crackers and Sulu," said George.

George and Harold ran to a window and looked out. There they saw their two evil twins sneaking home, carrying their beloved pets with them.

"Sulu and Crackers have no idea what's going on," said George. "They think those two guys are US!"

"How in the world are we going to stop *US*?" asked Harold.

CHAPTER 10

HYPNO-HORROR

George and Harold knew exactly where those evil twins had taken Crackers and Sulu. To the same place *they* would have taken them: their tree house.

So our two heroes dashed home as fast as they could. Then they climbed up the tree house ladder as *quietly* as they could.

But when they peeked inside, they saw
something that was three hundred and eighty-
nine times worse than they ever could have
imagined. Their evil twins were *hypnotizing*
their beloved pets with a 3-D Hypno-Ring.

"You will obey our every command," said
Evil Harold.

"Yeah," said Evil George. "And you'll be
really wicked from now on, too!"

George and Harold gasped, which is actually
not a very smart thing to do if you're trying
to go unnoticed.

"Hey, *LOOK*!" shouted Evil Harold. *"GASPERS!"*

"GET 'EM!" shouted Evil George to their newly hypnotized pets.

Crackers didn't move. The dazed pterodactyl shook his head and looked a little confused. But Sulu immediately sprung into action. He lunged at George and Harold, grabbed them by their shirts, and yanked them to the ground.

"Hey!" said Evil George. "Those kids look just like us. What should we do with them?"

"We can't take any chances," said Evil Harold. Then he called to Sulu in a loud and commanding voice, "DESTROY THEM, O WICKED HAMSTER!"

CHAPTER 11
CRACKERS TO THE RESCUE

Crackers did not understand what was going on, but the plucky pterodactyl knew that something needed to be done . . . and *quickly*. So with a sudden whoosh of flapping wings, Crackers swooped in and grabbed George and Harold from the relentless little paws of their raging robotic rodent rival.

"Oh, NO!" screamed Harold. "Crackers is going to fly us high into the air and drop us! We're DOOMED!"

"Actually, I think *he's* trying to *rescue* us," said George.

"But *he* got hypnotized just like Sulu," said Harold. "Why on Earth would *he* do the opposite of what *he* was ordered to do?"

"And how come all of our pronouns are getting italicized?" asked George.

"Let's not worry about that now," said
Harold. "We've gotta get out of here!"

"But we can't leave Sulu behind," cried
George.

"Don't worry," said Harold. "We'll come
back for Sulu!"

So the three friends flew to the school
and headed upstairs to the library.

"Hey! That looks like a pterodactyl," said
Mr. Krupp as our heroes pushed past him.
"Let me pet him! Let me pet him!" Mr.
Krupp cried, chasing after them.

George, Harold, and Crackers finally reached the library just in time to see Sulu and their evil twins smash through the ceiling with a terrible crash.

"You jerks won't get away from us *THIS* time," said Evil Harold.

Desperately, George, Harold, and Crackers tumbled into the Purple Potty, slammed the door shut, and quickly reset the controls.

Mr. Krupp and Sulu pounded on the door of the Purple Potty, while George and Harold's evil twins shook the malfunctioning time machine from side to side.

All at once, an orange light started flashing wildly. The Purple Potty began to shake and wobble violently. Then the entire room lit up with an explosive burst of lightning as the Purple Potty (and everyone around it) disappeared into a whirlwind of electric air.

PURPLE POTTY CO.

CHAPTER 12

KA-BLAMSKI!

Suddenly, there was another blinding flash
of light. Everyone around the Purple Potty
flew off in different directions. Then the
Purple Potty stopped shaking and wobbling,
and switched into shut-down mode.

Inside the image, on a sign: READING MIGHT OFFEND YOU ...Why TAKE A CHANCE?

George, Harold, and Crackers peeked out.

"Look," said Harold. "There aren't any books in this library. We must be back in our own reality."

"But we've got to be sure," said George.

The two boys tucked Crackers into Harold's book bag and crept out into the hallway. As they peered into the windows of nearby classrooms, they saw room after room of heartbroken and despondent-looking children.

Some were standing in corners, weeping . . . others were sitting on dunce stools wearing humiliating hats . . . while still others were writing unbelievably degrading sentences over and over on the chalkboard as their teachers rifled through their lunch boxes, stealing all of the best desserts.

"Yep," sighed George, "we're back in our own reality."

"I never thought I'd say this," said Harold, "but it's good to be home."

"To the tree house!" cried George.

CHAPTER 13

PURPLE POTTY PEOPLE UNITE!

Seconds after George, Harold, and Crackers left the library, four confused beings from an alternate dimension began to stir. Evil George, Evil Harold, Evil Sulu, and Nice Mr. Krupp stumbled to the center of the strange, empty library, rubbing their heads and looking around curiously.

"Look," said Evil George. "This library has no books on the shelves."

"Hmmmm," said Evil Harold. "It looks like we've entered some kind of alternate universe. An illogical reality where everything is backwards."

"Backwards, eh?" said Evil George. "*WE* could do quite well in a place like this!"

He walked over to the drinking fountain and splashed some water on Nice Mr. Krupp's face.

75

Suddenly, Nice Mr. Krupp's confused
smile turned into an evil frown. He ripped
off his clothes and tied a curtain from a
nearby window around his neck. Then Evil
George handed him a bad toupee, and the
pernicious principal stood before them,
snarling angrily through his flared nostrils.

"I AM CAPTAIN BLUNDERPANTS!" he
shouted in a thunderous voice.

CHAPTER 14

THE CHAPTER WHERE SOME STUFF HAPPENS

Meanwhile, back at their tree house, George and Harold grabbed some supplies before heading off to save Sulu.

"We'll need our 3-D Hypno-Ring," said George, "to change Sulu back to his old self again."

"Cool!" said Harold. "And we better take the rest of this Extra-Strength Super Power Juice, just in case."

"Good idea," said George.

The two friends stuffed their supplies and their pet pterodactyl into their book bags and headed down the tree house ladder.

"Just where the heck do you two think you're going?" asked a commanding voice at the bottom of the ladder. It was George's dad, and he didn't seem very happy.

"Uh," said George, "we-we need to go back to school for something."

"Yeah," said Harold. "We forgot something."

"Well, it'll have to wait until tomorrow," said George's dad. "We're having dinner with the Hutchinses tonight, remember?"

"Oh yeah," said George. "It's Grandparents Day. We almost forgot."

"Well, you're just in time for dinner," said George's dad. "Go inside and wash up."

"But the fate of the entire world is in our hands!" cried Harold.

"The fate of the entire world can wait until tomorrow," said George's dad.

CHAPTER 15
SUPER SUPPER

After they washed their hands, the two boys
went to the dining room. George's parents
had prepared a big meal, and everybody
waited patiently for George and Harold to
join them. Harold's mom, sister, and grandpa
were there, along with George's mom, dad,
and his great-grandma.

"Hello, babies," said George's great-grandma. "What have you boys been up to today?"

"Nothin'," said George as he hugged his great-grandma.

"We made you and Grandpa a comic book yesterday," said Harold.

"You did?" said Harold's grandpa. "Well, let's have a look!"

George shuffled through his book bag, taking things out and laying them on the table. "It's here somewhere," he said. Finally, he pulled out two copies of their latest comic book, "The Adventures of Boxer Boy and Great-Granny Girdle."

"It's about how you guys turn into superheroes and save the world and stuff," said George.

"I drew the pictures," said Harold.

"Well, that's very nice, boys," said George's dad. "Now sit down, and let's eat."

"We *can't*!" said George. "We've got to go now. It's really important!"

George and Harold's grandparents poured themselves a glass of juice and began reading their new comic books, while the boys continued arguing with George's dad.

THE ADVENTURES OF
BOXER BOY
AND
GREAT-GRANNY GIRDLE

By George Beard and Harold Hutchins

EveryBody Knows That Grandparents are Kinda dorky...

They tell dumb Jokes...

Why did the Silly-Willy Throw his clock in The air?

He wanted to see time FLY! Haw-Haw.

? ?

They call you embaressing NickNames in PubLick...

Hello, Babies!

Ha-Ha!

And They have no sence of what things cost.

Heres a nickel. Why dont you Buy a video game with it?

Thanks, I will.

5¢

But Grandparents are still cool **FOR ONE REASON.**

Were OLD!

And we don't care what Anyone Thinks!

outta my way, Buster Brown!

step aside, you Bother me!

our Heros!

SHOVE

WHACK

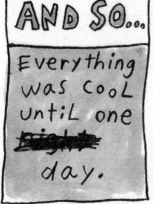

AND SO... Everything was cool until one ~~night~~ day.

when a strange new store opened up downtown.

RoBo-Geezers INC.

They were selling ROBOTS!

Hey Kids! TRade in your old, worn out grandparents FoR The Latest in ROBO-Geezer Tecknoligy!!!

Cool!

They're Tons Better Than Reguler grandparents

They tell Funny Jokes!

whats 40 Feet Long and smells Like Pee?

Line-dancers at the old Folks Home.

Ha-Ha

They call you cool Nicknames in PuBlick...

Hey ThoR!

Yo-what up, Dog?

And Best of all, They have no sense of what things cost.

Here's ten thousend dollers for a candy Bar.

ANYWAY...

One Day, George and Harolds Grandparents went downtown.

Something Fishy is going on in There.

Hmm

ROBO-Geezers INC.

So they snuck inside The Building.....

Shhh.

KEEP OUT

SOON....

Hey Look!

SLAVE Room

They opened the door and saw a Tragick discovery.

Hey! All of the grandparents in Town ~~could~~ Got turned into Slaves!

Oh, my

The Bad guys Ran upstairs

They got into a U.F.O. on Top of there Building.

ROBO GEEZERS

And took off.

ROBO

Calling all Robo Geezers! Attack Boxer Boy and Great Granny Girdle!

Suddenly, all the Robo-Geezers in Town Transformed.

Click Click

...And off they Flew.

The Robo-Geezers attacked. But Boxer Boy and Great Granny Girdle were...

Faster than a speding electric scooter...

More Powerful than adult diapers...

and able to Leap Tall buildings without Breaking a hip!!!

The RoBo-Geezers tried to devour the spaceship in a [■■■] wild feeding frenzy.

They ate and ate and ate and ate...

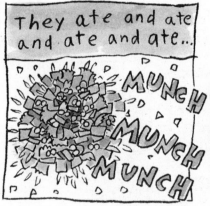

MUNCH
MUNCH
MUNCH

Then one of them bit on the fuel line.

AND

KA BOOM

CHAPTER 17

MEANWHILE, BACK AT THE TREE HOUSE . . .

While George and Harold pleaded with George's dad to be excused from dinner, a pack of evil thugs was just outside their window, sneaking up into their tree house.

"We've got to create some kind of diversion while we unleash our sinful scheme," said Evil Harold. The villains looked around the tree house for anything they could use.

"What's this little thing?" said Evil George. He pressed the button on the back of the miniature Goosy-Grow 4000. Suddenly, a beam of energy shot out of the tiny contraption, accidentally zapping Evil Sulu, who was tucked inside Evil Harold's shirt pocket.

Immediately, Evil Sulu began to grow
bigger and bigger until he leaped out of Evil
Harold's pocket and fell to the floor with a
giant *THUD*! Evil Sulu was now the size of a
full-grown sheepdog. The villains all smiled
at one another as they watched Evil Sulu
growl and snarl ferociously.

"I think we've found our diversion," said Evil George, as he zapped Evil Sulu again.

CHAPTER 18

CRASH !

Suddenly, Evil Sulu grew to the size of a giant monster. He jumped out of the tree house and landed in George's backyard with a terrible, thunderous crash.

"What was that?" cried George's dad.

Everyone jumped up and dashed
outside to get a better look at the horrible
creature that towered over the house,
snarling and roaring hideously. For some
strange reason, George and Harold's
grandparents jumped up and dashed the
fastest — faster than they had moved in

years—but nobody really noticed because
of the giant hamster thing.

"What's going on?" cried Harold.

"Those evil guys must have followed
us back to our own reality somehow,"
whispered George. "We've gotta stop them
before they take over OUR WORLD!"

Sulu crashed and smashed his way through the neighborhood, heading toward the big city . . . because, well, that's where giant monsters usually head. George ran inside and grabbed the 3-D Hypno-Ring and the Super Power Juice (which felt surprisingly empty), and whistled for Crackers. And while the grown-ups were fussing and fretting over trivial things like broken fences, insurance policies, and property-damage reports, George, Harold, and Crackers flew off to save the world.

CHAPTER 19

WHENHAMSTERSATTACK.COM

Soon the three friends soared over the center of the city. There they met up with their beloved pet, Sulu, who was now a giant, evil monster destroying everything in his path.

"Well," said Harold, "it looks like you
and I are going to have to drink that Super
Power Juice so we can stop Giant Evil Sulu
from wrecking the city."

"Uh, Harold?" said George, as he eyed the
carton of Super Power Juice suspiciously.

"I'm so *psyched*!" said Harold. "I've always
wanted to have super powers!"

"Uh . . . *Harold*?" said George again,
as he held the carton to his ear and
shook it back and forth.

"I hope I get Kung-Fu Grip . . . and X-ray vision!" said Harold. "That would be awesome!"

"Uh . . . *HAROLD*???" shouted George, as he turned the Super Power Juice carton upside down. "There's nothing left."

"What do you mean?" cried Harold. "There was, like, a *third* of a carton in there twenty minutes ago!"

"Well, it's gone now," said George. "It must have evaporated or something."

The boys watched helplessly as Giant Evil Sulu continued trashing the city.

"Well," said George, "I guess there's just one thing left to do."

Hurriedly, the three friends flew to the house of their principal, Mr. Krupp. It was easy to find, since it was the only house on Curmudgeon Boulevard that was covered in toilet paper.

"Next time we've gotta use single-ply toilet paper," said George. "We'll get better coverage."

After a quick knock on the door, and an even quicker snap of the fingers, Mr. Krupp transformed into the Amazing Captain Underpants. And in no time at all, the world's greatest, baldest superhero was face-to-face with the world's biggest, baddest bionic hamster.

CHAPTER 20

THE INCREDIBLY GRAPHIC VIOLENCE CHAPTER, PART 1 (IN FLIP-O-RAMA™)

PILKEY® BRAND
D-RAMA

HERE'S HOW IT WORKS!

STEP 1
First, place your *left* hand inside the dotted lines marked "LEFT HAND HERE." Hold the book open *flat*.

STEP 2
Grasp the *right-hand* page with your right thumb and index finger (inside the dotted lines marked "RIGHT THUMB HERE").

STEP 3
Now *quickly* flip the right-hand page back and forth until the picture appears to be *animated*.

(For extra fun, try adding your own sound-effects!)

FLIP-O-RAMA 1

(pages 115 and 117)

Remember, flip *only* page 115.
While you are flipping, be sure you
can see the picture on page 115
and the one on page 117.
If you flip quickly, the two
pictures will start to look like
<u>one</u> *animated* picture.

Don't forget to
add your own sound-effects!

LEFT HAND HERE

HAMSTER HAVOC

RIGHT
THUMB
HERE

HAMSTER HAVOC

FLIP-O-RAMA 2

(pages 119 and 121)

Remember, flip *only* page 119.
While you are flipping, be sure you
can see the picture on page 119
and the one on page 121.
If you flip quickly, the two
pictures will start to look like
<u>one</u> *animated* picture.

Don't forget to
add your own sound-effects!

LEFT HAND HERE

**PUT YOUR HEAD
ON MY BOULDER**

119

RIGHT
THUMB
HERE

PUT YOUR HEAD ON MY BOULDER

CHAPTER 21

THE ANTI-CLIMACTIC CHAPTER

The battle between man and beast was over. George and Harold petted Sulu's giant face and breathed a sigh of relief.

"He'll be O.K.," said George. "He just got knocked out."

"Great!" said Harold. "It looks like all of our problems are over!"

"NOT SO FAST!" said a voice that came from somewhere on the lower right-hand corner of the next page.

It was Evil George, along with Evil Harold and the Ultra-Evil Captain Blunderpants.

The terrible trio had been busy working on their preposterous plight (which is just a fancy way of saying that they were busy robbing a bank).

"Somebody's been messing with our giant attack hamster," said Evil Harold. "I think we need to teach those goody-goodies a lesson!"

"And I'm just the guy to do it!" said Captain Blunderpants proudly.

Instantly, the mood shifted. Everyone
stood back. The air crackled with tension. The
showdown of the century was about to begin.
Captain Underpants would soon engage in a
historic battle with his evil twin. Never before
had our brave hero encountered an enemy
who was so powerful. Pound for pound, super
power for super power, Captain Underpants
was pitted against his equal. He had met his
match. It was to be the ultimate smackdown
. . . an all-out war . . . the brawl to end all
brawls . . . the definitive clash between good
and evil . . . a momentous confrontation of
the most critical —

George snapped his fingers, and suddenly the horrifyingly evil Captain Blunderpants transformed into a friendly elementary school principal.

"Awww, maaaaaan!" cried Evil George and Evil Harold.

"We read your comic book back in chapter 8," said Harold. "Didja think we wouldn't remember how to turn your evil super-villain back into a harmless principal?"

George and Harold quickly found some
rope and tied up Evil George, Evil Harold,
and Nice Mr. Krupp. "We're taking you losers
back to your own reality where you won't
bother us ever again!" said George.

"All we have to do is de-hypnotize and
shrink Sulu, and our job will be done!" said
Harold. "Nothing can possibly go wrong now!"

"Y'know, you really shouldn't say things
like that," said George.

"Why?" said Harold.

CHAPTER 22
KA-BOOM!

Suddenly, lightning flashed, thunder crashed, and the rain came a-tumbling down.

"That's why!" said George.

As the first few drops of rain hit Captain Underpants's pudgy face, he began to transform. In a matter of seconds, he changed from a confident, powerful superhero into an angry, annoyed elementary school principal.

Unlikewisely, the rain-on-the-face thing was having the opposite effect on Nice Mr. Krupp, transforming him, once again, into an arrogant, foul-tempered super-villain named Captain Blunderpants.

Evil George and Evil Harold smiled their evilest smiles as Captain Blunderpants snapped their ropes and yelled out a triumphant "La-La-Traaaaa!"

George and Harold quickly snapped their fingers again and again, but it was having no effect. It was raining too hard, and Mr. Krupp was getting annoyed.

"This is the dumbest dream I've ever had!" he shouted. "I'm gonna go home and get back into bed." And with that, he turned and stormed off toward his soggy toilet-paper-covered house.

"Looks like the tables have turned," Evil
Harold snickered.

"You guys haven't won yet," said George.
Quickly, George and Harold leaped onto
Crackers's back, and the three forlorn friends
flew off toward their tree house.

"Don't just stand there!" cried Evil Harold
to his creepy cohorts. "LET'S GET 'EM!"

CHAPTER 23

TWO MINUTES LATER...

Back in George's yard, our heroes searched
furiously through their tree house.

"I found it!" cried George. "The Shrinky-
Pig 2000! All we have to do is shrink those
evil losers, and we'll save the world!"

"Too late!" shouted Captain Blunderpants as he grabbed George and Harold by their shirt collars.

"We'll take that 'Shrinky-Thingy,'" said Evil Harold, as the contraption slipped out of George's arms. "I'm not sure how it works, but once I figure it out, I can think of about *a million and nine* evil things to do with it!"

Captain Blunderpants held George and
Harold high in the air and snarled viciously.

"Prepare to be PULVERIZED!" he shouted.

"We're *DOOMED*!" screamed Harold.

"NOW WAIT JUST A COTTON-PICKIN'
MINUTE, YOUNG FELLA!" shouted a
familiar-sounding voice from inside George's
house. . . .

CHAPTER 24

NOBODY MESSES WITH OUR GRANDBABIES!

Harold's grandpa and George's great-grandma stepped out onto the back patio and confronted the big bully, Captain Blunderpants.

"You put those babies down or you'll get the whuppin' of your lifetime," said George's great-grandma.

Captain Blunderpants laughed haughtily.

"We're not going to warn you again, Skippy," said Harold's grandpa.

Captain Blunderpants continued to tighten his grip on George and Harold.

So the two octogenarians joined hands, gazed fiercely into each other's eyes, and shouted, "Geezer Powers *ACTIVATE*!"

Quickly they began spinning around and around. Faster and faster the old folks twirled until a tornado formed around them, tearing away their clothes and jewelry, and sending patio furniture flying violently.

Suddenly, the twirling stopped, the
tornado subsided, and the elderly twosome.
stood proudly in their underwear, huffing,
puffing, and fearlessly facing their foe.

"Oooh, that was fun. Let's do it again,
Henry," said George's great-grandma.

"Heh-heh," laughed Harold's grandpa. "Alright, my dear, but we've gotta teach that fat boy a lesson first."

"Oh yeah," said George's great-grandma. "That young fella's got a hankerin' for a spankerin'!"

Harold's grandpa grabbed a couple of curtains from the kitchen window and tied them around their necks. "Not too tight, Henry," said George's great-grandma.

With their capes in place, George and Harold's super-grandparents approached Captain Blunderpants triumphantly.

"Alright, sonny," said Harold's grandpa. "Prepare to get your bucket whupped by Boxer Boy and Great-Granny Girdle!"

CHAPTER 25

THE INCREDIBLY GRAPHIC VIOLENCE CHAPTER, PART 2 (IN FLIP-O-RAMA™)

FLIP-O-RAMA 3

(pages 143 and 145)

Remember, flip *only* page 143.
While you are flipping, be sure you
can see the picture on page 143
and the one on page 145.
If you flip quickly, the two
pictures will start to look like
<u>one</u> *animated* picture.

Don't forget to
add your own sound-effects!

LEFT HAND HERE

THE GERIATRIC
JAWBREAKER

RIGHT THUMB HERE

THE GERIATRIC
JAWBREAKER

FLIP-O-RAMA 4

(pages 147 and 149)

Remember, flip *only* page 147.
While you are flipping, be sure you
can see the picture on page 147
and the one on page 149.
If you flip quickly, the two
pictures will start to look like
<u>one</u> *animated* picture.

Don't forget to
add your own sound-effects!

LEFT HAND HERE

A CANE
IN THE BRAIN

RIGHT
THUMB
HERE

148

A CANE
IN THE BRAIN

FLIP-O-RAMA 5

(pages 151 and 153)

Remember, flip *only* page 151.
While you are flipping, be sure you
can see the picture on page 151
and the one on page 153.
If you flip quickly, the two
pictures will start to look like
<u>one</u> *animated* picture.

Don't forget to
add your own sound-effects!

LEFT HAND HERE

TAKE A WALKER
ON THE WILD SIDE

RIGHT
THUMB
HERE

TAKE A WALKER
ON THE WILD SIDE

CHAPTER 26

SHRINKY-DORKS

"Y'know," said George, "I think I just figured out what happened to the Super Power Juice that disappeared earlier."

"Oh yeah?" said Evil George. "But you didn't figure *THIS* out! All we have to do is press ONE BUTTON on this shrinking machine, and you'll all be transformed into tiny little shrimps!"

"Go ahead and press the button!" laughed Harold. "You're holding it backwards anyway. You'll just shrink yourselves!"

"Really?" said Evil Harold. "Gee, thanks!" He turned the Shrinky-Pig 2000 around and pressed the button.

And they were shrunk to the size of potato chips.

"Hey!" shouted Mini Evil George. "What happened?"

"Oops," said Harold. "I guess I made a mistake. You actually *WERE* holding it right the first time. My bad."

"Y'know," said George, "I think I know two little boys who could really use a good spanking!"

CHAPTER 27

THE INCREDIBLY GRAPHIC VIOLENCE CHAPTER, PART 3 (IN FLIP-O-RAMA™)

LEFT HAND HERE

HAPPY
SPANKSGIVING

159

160

HAPPY
SPANKSGIVING

CHAPTER 28

WRAPPING THINGS UP

"Well, it looks like our job here is done," said Boxer Boy.

"Yes, it is, my big strong man," said Great-Granny Girdle, giggling gleefully.

George and Harold looked at each other in horror.

"Y'know, little lady," said Boxer Boy, "somewhere out there is an all-you-can-eat buffet with a *Senior Citizens' Early-Bird Special* just going to waste!"

"Well, let's go find
it, you big hunk-o-love!"
said Great-Granny Girdle as she kissed
him passionately on his wobbly neck fat.

The scene that followed could best be
described as the drooliest five-minute kiss
in the history of children's books. Dentures
sloshed, wrinkles flapped, and rubbery
jowls squished, smooshed, and quivered
gelatinously.

"Ummm," said Harold, "I think I need to
go wash my eyeballs."

"Me, too," said George.

And as the Arthritic Avengers flew off into
the sunset, George and Harold decided to
try very, VERY hard not to think about the
disgusting event they had just witnessed.

"C'mon, we've gotta wrap this story up,"
said George. "First we need to de-hypnotize
and shrink Sulu."

"Then we've gotta go back into that crazy
Purple Potty and return these bozos to their
alternate universe," said Harold.

CHAPTER 29

TO MAKE A LONG STORY SHORT

ZAP!

CHAPTER 30

TO MAKE A LONGER STORY EVEN SHORTER

KICK!

CHAPTER 31

THE CHAPTER WHERE NOTHING BAD HAPPENS

"Gee, that worked out pretty good," said Harold. "Sulu is now back to his normal size and personality, and the Purple Potty People are back in their own reality where they won't be able to bother us ever again. I guess everything worked out perfectly!"

"Yeah, *nice going*," said George, looking a bit annoyed. "Why do you have to say things like that?"

"Things like *what*?" asked Harold.

"Haven't you been paying attention in these stories?" asked George. "Every time somebody says something like that, it always means that a buncha bad stuff is just about to happen."

"But what could possibly go wrong now?" asked Harold.

"*FREEZE!*" shouted the Chief of Police. "You guys are under arrest for robbing Frank's Bank. Looks like you're going to jail for the rest of your lives!"

"See what I mean?" said George. "You've gotta stop saying stuff like that!"

"I guess you're right," said Harold. "But at least things can't get any worse."

"Aaaaugh!" shouted George. "You did it *again*! Now I bet when you turn the page, something even *worse* is going to happen! You've gotta learn to keep your mouth shut at the end of these books!"

"Yeah, but what could be worse than going to jail for the rest of our lives?"

CHAPTER 32

THE THING THAT COULD BE WORSE THAN GOING TO JAIL FOR THE REST OF THEIR LIVES

Suddenly, out of nowhere, a ball of blue lightning appeared, growing bigger and bigger, until it exploded in a blinding flash.

And there, standing where the ball of lightning had been, was a smoking pair of giant robotic pants.

"This can't be good," said George.

A small opening at the front of the robo-pants began to unzip. And out of that opening peeked a fearsomely familiar face.

"Hey! It's Professor Poopypants!" shouted Harold.

The cops started to laugh.

"Stop LAUGHING!" shouted the little man peeking out of the giant zipper. "My name is no longer Professor Poopypants. I changed it to Tippy Tinkletrousers!"

The cops laughed even harder.

"And I've got a *special surprise* for anybody
who thinks my NEW name is funny!" said the
furious professor.

Immediately, the metallic pants opened up
at the top, and a giant laser shooter rose from
its robotic depths.

A brilliant burst of energy zapped the laughing cops, and suddenly they were both transformed into frozen statues.

"My Freezy-Beam 4000 will take care of anybody who stands in my way!" said Tippy. "And now," he said with a wicked smile, "it's time for my *revenge*!"

"OH, NO!" screamed George.
"HERE WE GO AGAIN!" screamed Harold.